Oh No, Not Ghosts!

Richard Michelson

Illustrated by Adam McCauley

Harcourt, Inc.
Orlando Austin New York San Diego Toronto London

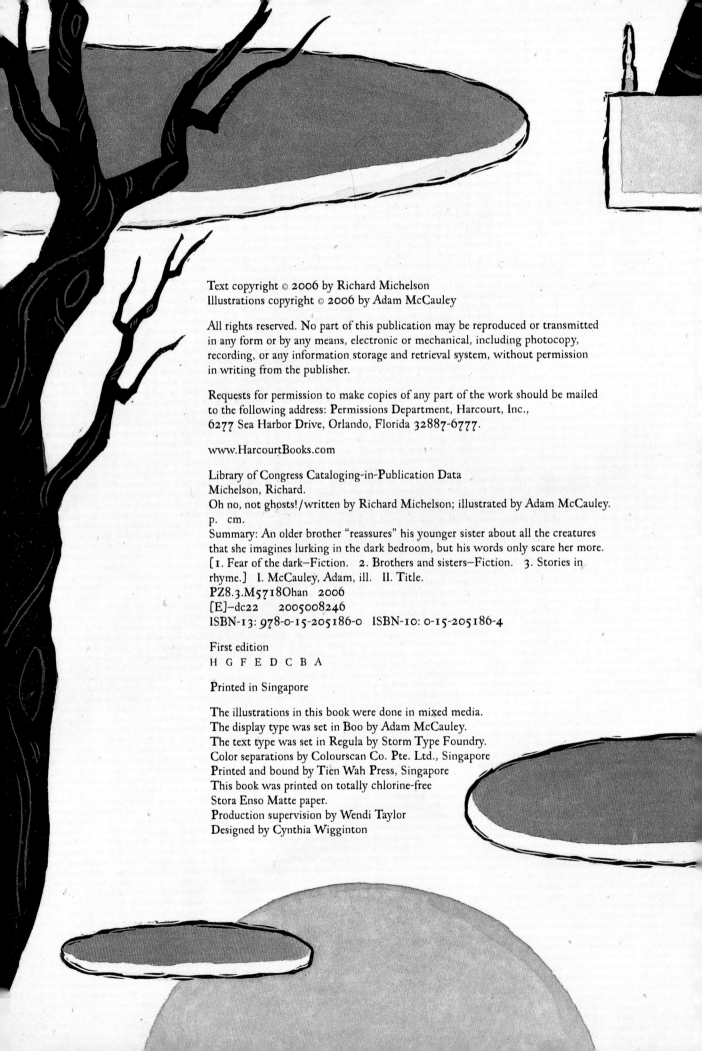

Requests for permission to make copies of any part of the work should be mailed
to the following address: Permissions Department, Harcourt, Inc.,
6277 Sea Harbor Drive, Orlando, Florida 32887-6777.

www.HarcourtBooks.com

Library of Congress Cataloging-in-Publication Data
Michelson, Richard.
Oh no, not ghosts!/written by Richard Michelson; illustrated by Adam McCauley.
p. cm.
Summary: An older brother "reassures" his younger sister about all the creatures
that she imagines lurking in the dark bedroom, but his words only scare her more.
[1. Fear of the dark—Fiction. 2. Brothers and sisters—Fiction. 3. Stories in
rhyme.] I. McCauley, Adam, ill. II. Title.
PZ8.3.M5718Ohan 2006
[E]—dc22   2005008246
ISBN-13: 978-0-15-205186-0 ISBN-10: 0-15-205186-4

First edition
H G F E D C B A

Printed in Singapore

The illustrations in this book were done in mixed media.
The display type was set in Boo by Adam McCauley.
The text type was set in Regula by Storm Type Foundry.
Color separations by Colourscan Co. Pte. Ltd., Singapore
Printed and bound by Tien Wah Press, Singapore
This book was printed on totally chlorine-free
Stora Enso Matte paper.
Production supervision by Wendi Taylor
Designed by Cynthia Wigginton

For my sister, Ellen, whom I NEVER...
well, hardly ever...okay, sometimes, teased—R. M.

For Maurice Sendak—A. M.

DON'T cry! Don't shout!

Don't make a peep.

I promised Dad

we'd let him sleep!

Shhhhhhhhhhhhh!

It's only wind.

Ignore that sound.

You're safe.

There are no ghosts around.

SHUSH!

There's no such thing as ghosts.

I guarantee it . . . well, almost.

Besides, if one sneaked up on you

and tried to scare you with a BOO,

I'd dress up like a werewolf,

ROoooooooooooar!

And scare that ghost

right through the door.

Werewolves? Oh no, not werewolves!

Quiet! There's no way that a werewolf's bite can turn kids into wolves at night.

And if it could, I'd stand defiant,

and bellow loud as twenty giants:

"Fee fee fi fi fo fo fum.

I eat werewolves. Yum Yum Yum."

HUSH!

Giants are **HUGE**. However . . .

they're also slow and not too clever.

It's okay that you're small and weak.

Be smart! Just make a high-pitched **Shrieek.**

I've seen a teeny demon frighten

the biggest, meanest, greenest titan.

Demons? Oh no, not demons!

QUIET down!

And stop that screamin'.

It's easy to scare off a demon.

Just paint your nose with pimples and warts
and stir a brew of smelly shorts.
Cackle, crackle, thwix, and thwax.
A witch turns demons into snacks.

RELAX.

There's not a thing to fear!

Do you see any broomsticks here?

Or pointed hats? Or YOWLLLing cats?

Or HISSSSing cauldrons? Or black bats?

Witches skedaddle and fly away

when skeletons come out to play.

Skeletons? Oh no, not skeletons!

SHUSH up!

Bones can't twirl and spin,

unless they're buttoned up with skin.

You'll learn that when

you're in first grade.

So quiet down—don't be afraid!

A skeleton's not half as bad

as a hairy, double-scary...

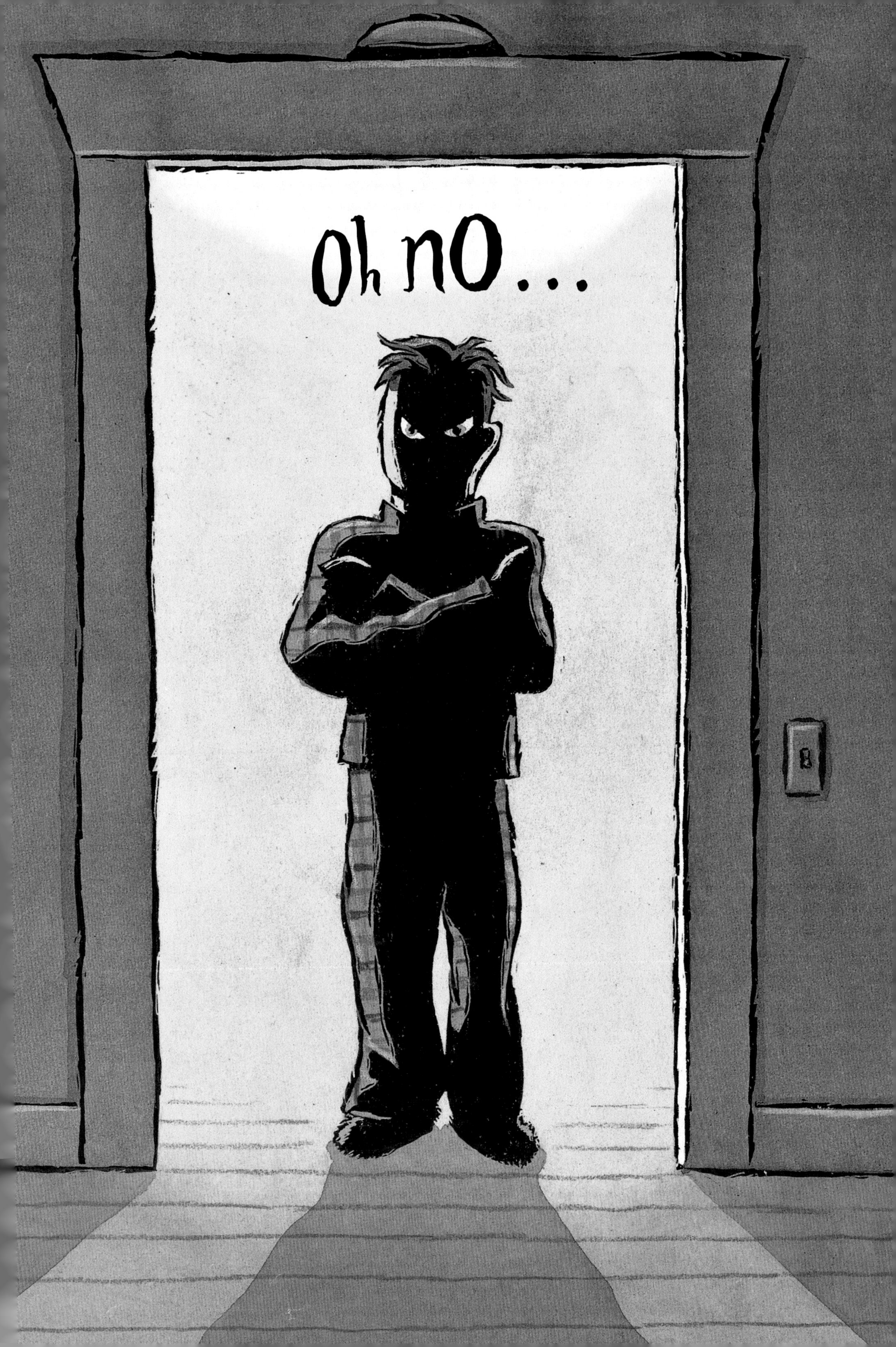
Oh nO...

not Dad!